WALT DISNEY PRODUCTIONS
presents

Scamp
Saves the House

Random House  **New York**

**GROLIER
BOOK CLUB EDITION**

First American Edition. Copyright © 1981 by Walt Disney Productions.
All rights reserved under International and Pan-American Copyright
Conventions. Published in the United States by Random House, Inc.,
New York, and simultaneously in Canada by Random House of Canada
Limited, Toronto. Originally published in Denmark as VAKS SLAR
ALARM by Gutenberghus Gruppen, Copenhagen. ISBN: 0-394-84817-9
Manufactured in the United States of America

1 2 3 4   C D E F G H I J K

The day of the dog show had arrived!

Jim and Darling were getting their dog, Lady, ready for the show.

Tramp, Lady's husband, was going to the show, too.

But Scamp had to stay home.

All of Lady's and Tramp's puppies had to stay home.

"Aunt Sara will look after you,"
said Darling. "Be good puppies now!"

Scamp, Fluffy, Ruffy, and Scooter
watched from the window while all of the
others drove away.

"Come down!" Aunt Sara cried. "You will get paw prints on the window."

Down jumped the puppies. Aunt Sara was very strict!

Then the puppies sat in front of
the fireplace.
They liked looking at the fire.

Scamp moved closer to the fire.
"Arf! Arf! Arf!" he barked.

Then he turned around
and wagged his tail.

Oops!
The fire burned the end of Scamp's tail.

"No, no!" scolded
Aunt Sara. "Do not
play with fire!"

Scamp hid under a chair.
He only came out when it was time to eat.

Soon Aunt Sara
fed the puppies.

Then she said, "It is time for our walk. Will you be good puppies?"

Fluffy, Ruffy, and Scooter barked happily.

They were always good.

"Arf!" added Scamp. He would try to be good, too.

Out they went.
Aunt Sara was
first.
    Then came Fluffy, Ruffy,
Scooter, and Scamp.

They walked by a big
puddle, but Scamp did not
jump into it.

A cat hissed at Scamp.
But he did not chase
after it.
He was being so good!

Soon they came to the fire station.

Scamp saw young firemen learning
how to put out a fire.

They were also learning how to
save people.

Scamp could not
resist.

He ran into the
firehouse yard.

He raced through
the spray from
the fire hose.

He ran up
the steps of
the training
tower. . . .

and jumped with a fireman
into the net below!

This is fun! thought Scamp
as he shook his wet fur.

The firemen laughed at the
silly puppy.

But then Scamp remembered
Aunt Sara and the other puppies.
They were marching away
down the street.

In the park, Aunt Sara stopped to count the puppies.

"One, two, three . . ."

Where was the fourth puppy? Where was Scamp?

Aunt Sara looked
behind bushes and trees.
"Scamp! Scamp!"
she called.

Along came a policeman.
"What is the trouble, Ma'am?" he asked.
"I should have four puppies," said
Aunt Sara. "But I only have three!"
Just then Scamp raced into line.

The policeman
counted the puppies.
"One, two, three,
four!"
"Four?" said Aunt
Sara.
There was Scamp,
right in line with
the others.

But he was
dripping wet!

"You bad dog!" Aunt Sara said angrily.
"You will sleep outside tonight, Scamp!"
And she made all the puppies turn around
and go home.

When they reached their house,
the puppies waited for Aunt Sara to
open the door.

Scamp hoped she would let him
come in.

But Aunt Sara remembered her promise.
"Out in the backyard with you!" she
said.

Poor Scamp!

Through the window he saw Fluffy, Ruffy, and Scooter having supper.

He saw them fall asleep in their warm, cozy bed.

He watched Aunt Sara
ironing her dress.

Soon she turned out the lights and
went to bed.

Poor Scamp lay down in his doghouse.
Suddenly he smelled smoke.
It was coming
from the house!

Scamp rushed to the window.
Aunt Sara had forgotten to turn off the iron.
The ironing board and the curtains were on fire!

The fire grew bigger and bigger.
Scamp had to do something.
He had to wake Aunt Sara!

"Arf! Arf! Arf!"
He barked as loudly
as he could.

Aunt Sara came to
her bedroom window.

"Be quiet, you bad puppy!"
she said.

She could not see
or smell the fire.

"Arf! Arf!" barked Scamp.

But Aunt Sara went
back to bed.

Then Scamp had
an idea.

He ran down the street
to the fire station.

"Arf! Arf!" he barked to the firemen.

"It is the puppy who played with us
today," said one fireman.

"But he is not
playing now,"
said another.

"He wants help!"

Scamp raced up the street.
He led the firemen to the
burning house.

The firemen used big hoses to put out
the fire.

One of the firemen picked Scamp up.

Aunt Sara and the puppies came
outside when they heard the noise.

"What are you doing?" asked Aunt Sara.

"Putting out the fire," said a fireman.

"This smart dog just saved your life!"

The next day, Jim
and Darling came home.
Lady had won first prize at the dog show!
She wore the prize medal on a ribbon
around her neck.

Everyone was very
proud of Lady.

Then Aunt Sara told them
about the fire.

She told how Scamp had
saved their lives.

Lady and Tramp smiled
at each other.

They were proud of Scamp.

Then Tramp took the
medal from Lady's neck and
gave it to Jim.

Jim knew what Tramp was thinking.
He put Scamp on a chair and tied
Lady's medal around Scamp's neck.
The family barked and cheered.

Scamp was a hero!
"What a wonderful puppy!"
said Aunt Sara.

Scamp felt proud and happy.
His house was safe and his
family was together again.